For Lucy

5 /7 25 278

HAMISH HAMILTON CHILDREN'S BOOKS
Published by the Penguin Group
27 Wrights Lane, London, W8 5TZ, England
Viking Penguin Inc., 40 West 23rd Street, New York, New York 10010, U.S.A.
Penguin Books Australia Ltd, Ringwood, Victoria, Australia
Penguin Books Canada Ltd, 2801 John Street, Markham, Ontario, Canada L3R 1B4
Penguin Books (N.Z.) Ltd. 182–190 Wairau Road, Auckland 10, New Zealand

Penguin Books Ltd, Registered Offices: Harmondsworth, Middlesex, England

First published in Great Britain 1989 by
Hamish Hamilton Children's Books

Copyright © 1989 by Adèle Geras
Illustrations copyright © 1989 by Frances Wilson
1 3 5 7 9 10 8 6 4 2

British Library Cataloguing in Publication Data
Geras, Adèle
Coronation picnic.
I. Title
823'.914[J]

ISBN 0-241-12554-5

Typeset in Baskerville by Wyvern Typesetting, Bristol
Printed in Great Britain at the University Press, Cambridge

Chapter 1

6 am

AMY HUGHES WOKE up while it was still dark and knew immediately what day it was. The last day of May: Sunday May 31st, 1953, and the day after tomorrow Princess Elizabeth would have her Coronation in Westminster Abbey in London. I wish, thought Amy, squinting through the gauzy white of her mosquito net at the map of the world pinned to her

1

bedroom wall, that we didn't have to
live so far away. It didn't look too bad
on the map: you could slide your
finger in a second across the smooth
paper from Great Britain, coloured
pink, down a little and across the

mauve and tan and lime green
countries of Africa, over a couple of
inches of blue and a few tiny islands
and another small stretch of water
that was the South China Sea and
you'd arrived. North Borneo. Your
finger could point to Jesselton and you
could say: that's where I live and it's
only a few inches away from London,
but really the distance was thousands
and thousands of miles. Amy had no
particular wish to go and live in
England, and didn't often think about
it, but the Coronation . . . It would
have been wonderful to see that, to
stand in the street and wave flags and
cheer as the new young Queen came
out of the Abbey.

Amy untucked the mosquito net,
got out of bed and turned on the light.

Looking out of the window and across the road, she could see that the Cranleighs' light was on too. Tonia was awake. Amy imagined all her friends getting ready: waking up and switching their lights on and preparing what they needed for the Coronation Picnic: Luise and Stefan Brucker in the big white house up on the hill, Tonia and Paul just over the road and Ian and Derek in the Robertsons' funny little house on the other side of the town.

Amy's Dad came into the room in his pyjamas.

"Up already, are you? Good show! Come and have some breakfast when you're dressed."

"I've been up for ages," Amy said. "So's Tonia."

Amy's Dad laughed. "Paul's probably putting the finishing touches to one of his famous treasure maps. Don't be too long now."

"OK."

Amy started dressing in her bathing costume and the shorts and blouse that she had put ready on her chair. I wish, she thought, that I had time to look at the scrapbooks today. Maybe when we get back from the picnic. The scrapbooks lived in the bottom

drawer of the chest of drawers and had belonged to Amy's mother. Now, they were Amy's most precious possession. They held photographs cut from hundreds of newspapers and magazines, which together recorded the life of the Royal Family and especially the lives of the princesses, Elizabeth and Margaret Rose. Amy's mother had given the scrapbooks to Amy two years ago and she had added everything she could possibly find to the collection. Now, as well as pictures of a smiling girl on the balcony of Buckingham Palace and a smart young lady in uniform, as well as wedding photographs and portraits of the new baby prince, there were sad pictures of King George VI's funeral, with his mother and wife and daughter all wearing black veils over their faces.

Sitting on the floor to put on her sandals, Amy thought about the day ahead and sighed. Picnics, and this Coronation Picnic more than any other, were supposed to be such a treat that she felt guilty about not really looking forward to it. I can't ever tell anyone, she said to herself. They'd think I was stupid, believing in ghosts at my age. I am stupid. Stupid to let a few sentences worry me. Luise probably didn't understand properly what her amah told her. And anyway maybe her amah was making it up to frighten her. Amy remembered it all very clearly. One day when Mrs Aston was teaching the children about what had happened in

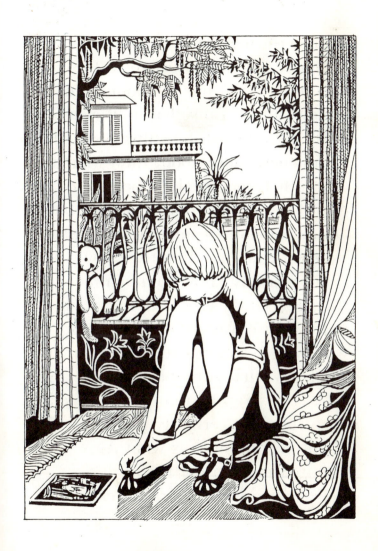

Borneo during the War, when the Japanese forces had occupied the Colony and put lots of people into prison camps, Luise had told everyone what she'd heard. She always acted as if she knew more about things like this than other people: she'd been born in one of the camps, that was true, but as she was only a tiny baby when the War ended, Amy didn't see how she could possibly know so much more than everybody else.

But Luise was the sort of person who was so sure about all the things she knew, that Amy believed her and took it for granted that what she said was true. The certainty that Luise felt about everything was what Amy admired most in her friend.

Perhaps Mr and Mrs Brucker,

Luise's parents, told her about that time. Perhaps because they were German and had come to Borneo to run away from Hitler even before the War began, they really *did* know more than other people. Anyway, they'd all been talking about the War when Luise had said, "My amah says that some people tried to live on Gaya Island. She says it's haunted by ghosts. Women and children, who went there to hide and then couldn't ever get back, but died on the island."

Mrs Aston had scoffed at the idea of ghosts, but didn't deny the fact that some people may indeed have died.

"But we go there for picnics!" Amy had burst out, in front of all the class. "How can we go there for picnics when people have died there?"

Ian and Derek and Tonia and Luise
had laughed out loud.

"Silly!" said Ian. "People have died
everywhere, all over the world. You
are silly, honestly. Someone's
probably died in the very spot where
you're sitting now . . . or where your
house is."

"I suppose so," Amy had said then,

agreeing that she'd been foolish, but now that they were about to go to Gaya Island for the picnic, the fear had begun to creep back. She shook her head. I don't believe in ghosts, she thought, and anyway, they'd never appear with a whole lot of us having a picnic there and in bright sunlight. There's nothing to be afraid of.

The darkness had vanished: pale apricot streaked the sky behind the black mass of the mountain, Kinabalu, that looked as though it were growing in Tonia's back garden.

"Are you coming for breakfast, dear?" shouted Amy's mother from the dining-room.

"Yes," Amy called back, and took her sunhat from the hook on the back of her door.

13

Chapter 2

8 am

ON THE LAUNCH going across to the island, Paul said, "I've brought a treasure map."

Everyone groaned. Tonia, who was older than her brother and used to defending him, said: "There's no need for you to groan like that. It's a perfectly good map, and it's fun

14

looking for treasure. You can't just swim and lie on the beach all the time."

Ian, who was ten and nearly ready to go to boarding-school in England, said, "Paul's treasure mad, that's the trouble. He's always on about his silly

old treasure, and it's not a perfectly good map at all. Maps are supposed to be *of* places, so that you can recognize them. That's just any old island Paul's drawn. He makes them up out of his head. And how does he know where there's any treasure anyway? Did he put it there? I think it's all stupid."

"You don't know," said Luise. "There could be treasure. We might find something . . . some of the people who were here during the War might have hidden something. Or we might find an unexploded bomb."

"If we *do* find something interesting," said Derek, who was a year younger than Ian and copied him in everything, "it won't be thanks to Paul's ridiculous little map. He's been

reading too many pirate stories, I expect."

Stefan, Luise's younger brother, laughed and kicked Paul playfully on

the shin. Stefan is always kicking people, Amy thought when she saw him doing it. He's often kicked me. He's never kicked Ian or Derek. He wouldn't dare. He doesn't kick Tonia any more either. Amy smiled as she remembered Tonia kicking Stefan back. He'd had a wonderfully yellow and purple bruise on his leg for ages. She wished that she had the courage to do something like that, but she'd never dared. She'd never even stuck out her tongue at Stefan behind his back. Partly she was frightened of Stefan himself, and partly she feared that Luise wouldn't want to be her friend any more if she went round attacking her younger brother. Amy looked at Paul. He had turned away and was pretending to gaze over the size of the launch, down into the water, but Amy could see that he was trying hard not to cry.

Luise said, "I think a treasure hunt's a very good idea. We could use

your map, Paul, and the first person
to find any kind of treasure wins . . .
sixpence."

"Right-o!" said Ian.

"Wizard!" said Tonia, and all at
once everyone had gathered around
Paul, discussing where to go and what
to look for, as if the funnily-shaped
drawing had suddenly become the
most accurate map in the whole

world. Amy looked at Luise and wondered what it was about her that made everybody – teachers, other children, all her friends – do almost exactly what she wanted.

When Amy first came to the school, Luise had been friendly to her and had included her in all the games and private talks that went on in the playground and for this Amy still felt grateful. It would have been dreadful to have been left out of everything.

There wasn't anything special about the way Luise looked. She was tall, with short, dark hair cut into a fringe. Tonia was prettier, with her long, golden plaits and big blue eyes, and she was better at dancing and running. Ian and Derek and even Stefan were stronger, and Ian was cleverer. Privately, Amy thought that she, too, was cleverer than Luise, and yet they all of them did just as Luise

suggested, and seemed to want nothing better than to please her and win her approval. But I like her, thought Amy. I can't help it. I like her and I wish I could be like her. She doesn't seem to be afraid of anything, and things are never boring when she's there. The most ordinary games turn into adventures. For a tiny moment, a horrible thought, a horrible wish flew into Amy's mind and buzzed there like a black insect: I wish that something would happen to Luise on Tuesday and then I could be Peter Pan in the dancing display. Amy pushed this thought firmly out of her head. Mrs James, their teacher, had been quite right to pick Luise as Peter Pan and Tonia as Wendy.

"You, Amy, are almost as tall as Luise, so you can be her understudy," she'd said. "Do you think you can learn the steps?"

Amy had nodded and learned the steps, and also her own steps as one of the pirates. They'd rehearsed and rehearsed. The display was going to be part of the Coronation celebrations.

The Governor was going to watch. There would be tea and cakes afterwards at the Club. Amy had never told anyone that she'd hoped to be chosen as Peter Pan, and most of the time she forgot all about it. It was just now and again that she found herself wishing . . . and then she felt guilty and wicked and told herself it didn't really matter about her. What mattered was that the display for the Coronation should be as good as it possibly could be. Everything had to be perfect for Coronation Day. Otherwise, she felt, it might spoil the occasion for Princess Elizabeth, all that way away in England.

Amy listened to the phut-phut-phut of the launch's engine as they drew nearer to the island. All the grown-ups – her parents, the Bruckers, the Cranleighs, the Robertsons, together with Stella Holloway, who was Mr Cranleigh's secretary and Ronnie Maine who was Stella's boyfriend – were laughing and drinking beer up near the bows of the launch. The children were sitting near the stern, on benches. Amy looked into the water, which was the colour of emeralds and completely clear from the surface right down to the sea-bed, where greeny-white sand had formed itself into rippling ridges far below them. She could see the light, hazy through the water, dappling small, pale coral forests and huge, freckled shells with pink hearts. Tiny silver fish flickered over the sand and occasionally a jellyfish blobbed past,

trailing innocent-looking transparent
tentacles that could sting you
dreadfully. Jesselton was growing
smaller and smaller behind them,
until only a white line showed where
the houses were, and behind them the
lower slopes of Kinabalu stretched up
and up through more shades of green
than Amy could count.

"Nearly there, kids!" Mr Robertson
called. "Gather your belongings."

The phut-phut-phut died away. The
launch was safely anchored and
everyone jumped into the water,
forming a line that led right onto the
beach.

"That's the ticket," said Amy's
Dad. "Here comes the food! Hurry
along now!"

Baskets of food and drink were

passed from hand to hand until they reached the spot which the ladies had chosen as Picnic Headquarters, in the welcome shelter of some trees, thickly hung about with creepers.

Chapter 3

10 am

"I FEEL," said Tonia, "like a fish in the market."

"You *do* smell a bit," Derek giggled.

Tonia picked up a handful of sand and threw it in what she thought was his direction. A gust of wind blew it onto Luise.

"Honestly, Tonia," she said. "Can't you look where you're chucking that stuff? I've got it all over me now."

"Go and rinse it off, then," Tonia said.

"I don't think I'm ever going to go in the water again." Luise sat up. "My toes look like prunes, only white. Amy, what do you think we should do? I'm fed up with just lying down all the time."

Amy lifted her head and looked around. Some of the grown-ups were still jumping about in the water. So were Ian and Stefan, although they seemed to be underwater rather a lot, only coming up for air from time to time. Her mother and Luise's mother were giggling. Stella and Ronnie had disappeared, probably trying to find somewhere where they could be alone together. Mrs Robertson was reading a book. Amy wondered how she could possibly concentrate in all this white sunlight and with everybody chattering and shouting all around her.

"I suppose we could start the treasure hunt," she said.

"Good idea," said Luise. "I'll go and get the boys and rinse my costume at the same time."

"But you said . . ." Tonia began.

"I didn't really mean it though, did I?" Luise made a face at Tonia and ran down to the water.

Amy sat up. She had been thinking about England, about what she remembered of London from the last time they'd been home on leave: grey skies and red buses and busy streets and people in dark clothes. Rain. Not

the torrential, monsoon rain of Borneo
that turned roads into small rivers
within minutes, but soft, polite, I'll-
fall-as-quietly-and-gently-as-I-can-so-
as-not-to-worry-you rain that ran
neatly into the drains and got soaked
up by all the streets and houses. She
looked at the curve of the beach: at
the sand like silvery powder, the
fringe of palm trees and creepers that
sheltered the ladies, and the turquoise
water that broke in frilly waves, edged
with a foam like lace. She saw the sky,
pale blue from above her head to the
horizon. She listened to the sucking
sounds of water on sand, the calling of
birds she couldn't identify, and the
voices of people rising into the
sunlight. It can't be true, she thought.
What Luise said can't be really true.

There can't be any ghosts here. It's too lovely.

Luise came running back up the beach, followed by Ian and Stefan.

"Right," she said, sinking to her knees in the sand. "Let's have a look at that map, Paul."

"I'll have to explain it to you," said Paul. "I've made a couple of things a bit different, now that I've seen what this bit of beach looks like . . . see?

This is where we are and the treasure
is there somewhere . . . near the
middle of the island. That's the rocks
over there," he pointed down the
beach, "and that's those trees over
there." He pointed in the opposite
direction. "The treasure," Paul looked
thoughtful for a moment, "is guarded
by a huge, scaly dragon, and it's in a
kind of hollow . . . in a tree, or a rock
or something like that."

"We'd better split up to look," said Derek, "and meet back here after an hour."

"We haven't got watches," Amy said.

"We'll borrow them from the grown-ups. They won't mind," said Ian. "Paul, you go over and explain. Tell them what we're doing."

Paul ran off down the beach to get as many watches as he could.

"I'll go with Tonia," said Luise, and Amy felt a sudden mixture of painful feelings: disappointment and anger and jealousy and a crossness towards Tonia, even though she'd done nothing. She'd only been chosen. Amy's common sense told her that Tonia was easily the best partner in a treasure hunt: she could climb trees better than any of the boys, but still, Amy felt as though a cloud had passed over the sun.

"I'll go with Stefan," said Derek.

Ian laughed. "So I'll go with either Paul or Amy," he said.

"You'd better all go together," Luise said. "Paul can't go on his own. Neither can Amy. Come on, let's get started. We'll meet here at twelve noon. Right?"

"Right," said Ian. "Follow me, Paul and Amy. We're going to the rocks. We'll be the ones to find the treasure, you'll see. Paul's the mapmaker, after all."

He set off down the beach with Paul running along beside him and Amy trailing sadly after them, looking down at her feet making squelchy marks in the wet sand. She liked Ian. Usually she would have been pleased to spend a whole hour with him, but she couldn't push from her mind the thought that if there was going to be one extra person, Paul could have gone with Ian and Luise could have asked her as well as Tonia. It could have been all the girls together. But Luise hadn't asked her. It hadn't even occurred to her.

"Come on, Amy," Ian shouted over his shoulder. "Buck up!"

Amy started to run.

"We've walked for miles," Ian said, sitting down on an old tree stump in a clearing, "and we haven't found a thing."

"What about the bottle?" said Paul.

"It's only an old beer bottle," said Amy, who was tired of looking for treasure and beginning to feel hungry.

"You don't know that," said Paul. "It might have had a message in it. A sailor might have thrown it overboard from far away."

39

"But we haven't got the message, have we?" said Ian. "So it doesn't count."

"Well," said Paul, "there's the shoe."

"It's only an old plimsoll, half rotted away," said Amy. "I don't think that counts as treasure. I say we should go back now. It's half past already."

"Let's just go a tiny bit further, it looks really mysterious up there. I'm sure we'll find something . . ." Paul stood up and began to push his way through the undergrowth.

"For goodness sake, Paul," said Ian, "look where you're going. There could be snakes or scorpions or anything . . ."

Ian followed Paul into the leaves.

"Come on, Amy," he called over
his shoulder.

Amy sighed and brushed her sandy
hands on her shorts. I wonder, she
thought, how the others are getting
on. It's very dark in here. The trees
are so thick overhead that you can't
see the sky, except in tiny pieces. I
hope Luise trips over a tree-root and

hurts her foot and then I can be Peter Pan . . . no, I don't wish that, really I don't. Amy closed her eyes, trying to get some proper thoughts into her mind, but it was no good. I'm not enjoying this picnic and it's a Coronation Picnic. I *should* enjoy it . . . but it's silly, all the time wandering about looking for treasure that isn't there. And I don't like it here. It's all green and wet. Paul and Ian aren't saying anything. They probably don't like it either. Suddenly, a terrible shrieking cry broke the silence and Amy felt as though the blood had stopped going round her body.

"What was that?" she managed to croak.

"Bird, I expect," said Ian. "Horrible noise, wasn't it?"

Amy couldn't speak. She nodded instead.

"I don't think it was a bird," said Paul. "I think it was the horrid scaly dragon, the one that guards the treasure."

"Then where is he?" said Ian.

Paul looked carefully at the tapestry of leaves and creepers and branches that hung down on both sides of the narrow path.

"There . . ." he whispered in triumph. "Look! There's the dragon."

Ian and Amy stood frozen into silence as the most enormous lizard they had ever seen crossed the path slowly, right in front of them.

"It's huge," breathed Ian. "Nearly three feet long, it must be."

Amy shuddered. "It's like a

dinosaur. It's horrible. I want to go back now."

"It's going," Ian said. "Don't be scared. I'm sure it can't hurt you. Look, it's gone." He sounded almost regretful.

"We can go back now," said Paul. "We've seen the dragon, and I bet that no one else has."

They followed the path back to the clearing.

"I'm starving," said Amy. She was so relieved that the lizard had disappeared, that the treasure hunt was nearly over, that it was lunchtime and above all that there hadn't been even a hint of a ghost that she forgave Luise for not choosing her as a partner.

As they climbed down from the rocks and began to walk along the beach, Ian said, "The others are all there already, and look, they're waving their hands like mad. Why do you think?"

"I bet they've found something,"

said Paul. "Treasure! Come on, let's go and see."

"Look!" Amy could hear Stefan shouting as they came closer. "Come on, you three. Look what I've found. It's better than treasure . . ."

Amy, Ian and Paul sank down into the sand. Stefan was hiding something behind his back.

"OK," said Ian. "Let's have a look at whatever it is."

Stefan held out his hand. He was cradling something smooth and white and rounded.

"It's a skull," he said. "I found a skull. A real one."

Chapter 4

12 noon

"I COULDN'T EAT even one more crumb," said Luise.

"Nor me," said Amy. "And anyway, there doesn't seem to be much left."

It was true. The small mountain of sandwiches, the little sausages out of tins, the mangoes, lychees and pineapples had disappeared. Bottles of lemonade and beer had been emptied and now stood in their crates waiting to be taken back to Jesselton. It had been a wonderful picnic lunch, and all the talk had been about the skull. Stefan had shown it first of all to his father, who was a doctor.

"Where did you find this?" Dr Brucker asked.

"It was in a hollow tree trunk," Derek said. "The tree had fallen on its side and this skull was just lying there. I saw the top of it first, sticking out."

"But I found it properly," Stefan was quick to point out. "I was the one who went and got it."

"Did you look to see if there were any . . ." Dr Brucker hesitated.

"Any other bones, do you mean?" Stefan said. "Yes, we did. But this is all there was. Is it real? Can you tell how old it is?"

"Not really. It's very small. Probably a child. It's hard to know exactly how old. Maybe five or six." Dr Brucker sighed. "It could be from the War, of course. That's most likely, I suppose, but it could be much older. What are you going to do with it, now that you've found it?"

"Bury it," said Luise immediately. 'We'll have a proper funeral, straight after lunch."

"Good," said Dr Brucker. "I think that would be the correct thing to do."

Stefan disagreed most fiercely with Luise and his father, and the rest of lunch turned into a long argument.

"It's not fair," said Stefan. "I found it, so it's mine. I think it's treasure and I want to keep it."

"It's not treasure," said Luise. "It's a skull. It used to be a person. How would you like to have your skull being used as an ornament or a souvenir or something by some oaf of a boy?"

"I'm not an oaf, and I wouldn't care, would I? I'd be dead."

"You have to bury it," said Amy, "otherwise the ghost of whoever it belonged to would be sad. It might even haunt you."

"I don't believe in ghosts, so there," said Stefan.

"I think," said Ian, "that we should vote on it. All those who want a proper funeral, raise your hands."

Five hands went up. Only Derek and Stefan were against the funeral.

"We have the funeral then," said

Ian. "That's what most people want."

Derek snorted rudely and Stefan looked furious.

"I think it's feeble," he shouted. "It won't be a proper funeral. We haven't got a proper graveyard or anything."

"It *will* be a proper funeral," said Luise, "so there. We'll say prayers and sing hymns and we'll even . . ." her eyes shone, "we'll even have a Coronation of our own, just like the *real* Coronation. That'll make the funeral really special and important. Amy can be the queen because she likes the real Queen so much."

"We know," Stefan crowed. "She cuts out all those soppy pictures of the stupid old princesses and sticks them in scrapbooks."

"Shut up, Stefan," said Luise, just as Amy opened her mouth, ready to defend Elizabeth and Margaret Rose. She thought better of it and said nothing.

"You don't know anything about it," Luise continued. "So shut up. We have to get ready."

Amy decided then and there to let Luise help her when she stuck the Coronation pictures into her album after the great day.

"What do we need?" asked Tonia.

"A crown," said Paul. "I'll make one out of a bit of creeper."

"I'll find a shell or something," said Tonia, "to be that thing the Queen's going to carry."

"A sceptre," said Amy. "Or an orb. That's the kind of round thing with jewels all over it. Mrs Aston said."

"That's it," said Tonia. "I'll go and find a really royal-looking shell."

"But you've got to have a robe or a
cloak or something," said Luise to
Amy. "You can't be crowned Queen
of Gaya Island without a robe." She
frowned.

"I know," said Amy, "we'll borrow
one of the towels and just tie it round
my neck."

"Can I be the Archbishop of
Canterbury?" asked Ian.

"I suppose so," said Luise. "As
you're the tallest. I'm the Queen
Mother, and Tonia can be Princess

Margaret Rose. I'll go and borrow some straw hats from the grown-ups and we can stick frangipani flowers into them."

Amy watched Luise gathering all the ladies' hats together and thought: she chose me to be Queen. Me. I'm sorry I ever wished that she would hurt her foot and I'm sorry I was so upset when she didn't choose me as a partner for the treasure hunt.

Chapter 5

2 pm

AMY HAD BEEN told to sit down on a log half-buried in the sand while the others sang a couple of hymns.

"You sit there," Luise said, "and when you hear us singing the first words of 'God save the King', or 'God save the Queen' I suppose we should say, you get up and walk very slowly right up to Ian and then he'll say something. He'll have to make it up, and then you'll get the crown put on and you can carry the shell that Tonia found. Right?"

"Right," said Amy and sat down to wait with a long white towel striped in red and blue tied round her neck. The towel belonged to the Bruckers.

"Frightfully patriotic," Mrs Brucker had said, laughing. It was very hot now. Amy was sitting in the shade, but the sun made patterns of light on the ground at her feet. Sweat ran down her neck and into the towel. The light was yellow now, thick and moist, with none of the freshness of the morning left in it. There was no wind at all. It seemed to Amy that every leaf and twig was unnaturally still, as if it had been put under a spell. All the others were some distance away, getting ready for the Coronation . . . and for the burial of the skull. Stefan was holding it. He would hold on to it, Amy knew, right up to the very moment it had to go into the ground. No one had brought a spade, but that didn't really matter. The ground was so sandy and soft that it was easy to dig holes in it with your hands. The voices of Luise, Tonia, Derek and Ian, Stefan and

Paul rose and fell in Amy's head like a kind of music, and even further away, someone was laughing. And all the time, the heat pressed down on Amy's head and shoulders, heavy and stifling. She noticed a small movement near one of the trees out of the corner of her eye. She turned. A small child

in a torn pink frock was looking at her
solemnly. This girl had her thumb in
her mouth. She was wearing red
plastic hairslides shaped like small
bows. Her long hair was parted in the
middle.

"Hello," Amy said.

The little girl said nothing.

"Pay attention, Amy," said Derek. "You look half asleep."

"Asleep? No, I wasn't. I saw somebody."

"Who?"

"There." Amy pointed to where the child had been standing, only seconds before.

"Nothing there now," said Derek, "and anyway, you *were* asleep. I saw you. You had your eyes closed when I came up to you."

"Did I?" Amy said. "I suppose I must have been, then. But it was so clear."

"A dream, I expect," said Derek. "What did you see?"

Surprisingly, Amy found that she didn't want to tell Derek anything about the girl. Perhaps she would tell

Luise later, but maybe not. Maybe the child's face and the red hairslides would remain her secret. But it had all been so clear. Surely it couldn't all have been just a dream?

"I've forgotten what it was now," she said to Derek. "Are they ready to start?"

"Yes," said Derek. "That's what I've come to tell you. We're going to begin."

"I'm ready," said Amy.

The children started singing. First they sang 'We three Kings' because, as Tonia said, it sounded royal. Then they sang 'Rock of Ages' because it was dignified. Amy listened. When the hymns were over, the first words of 'God save the Queen' rose into the air. Amy started walking slowly up

63

the path in as stately a way as possible. The red and blue and white striped towel hung down behind her and trailed on the sand. Luise had chosen the place well. Trees nearly met over her head as she walked. She pretended that she was really Princess Elizabeth, walking up the length of Westminster Abbey in a gown encrusted with jewels. As she knelt down in the sand and Ian put the wreath of creepers round her head, she remembered pictures Mrs Aston had shown them of the real crown, studded with gemstones the size of boiled sweets.

"Arise, Queen Amy," Ian said and Amy stood up. "Here is the Royal Shell of this island. Rule over us well."

Amy nodded as an enormous shell was placed in her hands. It was shaped like a spiral, going round and round in a pattern of black and brown stripes from the wide base to the pointed tip, and the inside of the shell was mother-of-pearl that shimmered and caught the light and changed its colours from pale grey to green and blue and pink every time you moved it.

"You have to turn round now," Paul said, "and walk all the way back again to where you were before and when you've done that, the Coronation bit is over and we can have the funeral."

As Amy walked back, everybody clapped and cheered. I'd forgotten all about the funeral, she thought, it was

such fun having my own Coronation
. . . Queen Amy. And then a thought
came into her mind quite suddenly
and swiftly, like a white bird flying up
out of the branches of a tree: the little
girl whom she had seen just a few
moments ago was the one whose skull
they were about to bury. She had seen
a ghost, she was quite sure of it. She
was just on the point of turning round
and telling everyone when something,
some feeling that she couldn't give a
name to, stopped her. All of a sudden
she didn't want anyone else to know.
They probably wouldn't believe her.
Derek would tell them she'd been
asleep. Maybe she had been asleep.
Maybe the child had been a kind of a
dream. Perhaps that's all they were
really, all those ghosts that people

said they'd seen, like dreams, only more solid. The girl had looked so real. Amy could remember the smocking on the front of her frock and the red plastic bows in her hair.

"Are you coming, Amy?" shouted Luise.

"Yes, I'm just taking this towel off. I'm so hot."

Amy untied her queenly train and left it lying on the ground, but she didn't take her crown off, nor did she put down the shell which seemed to her like a treasure and something she could keep to remind herself of the day when she'd been Queen Amy, just for a bit.

Paul and Derek had dug a hole. Everyone stood round in silence while the skull was laid in it.

"It looks funny," said Paul. "Sort of empty."

"What can we put in, though?" asked Ian. "There's nothing I can think of."

"If we'd known," said Tonia, "that we were going to find it, we could have brought something from home."

"I know," said Amy. "She can have my crown." She put the wreath of rather droopy-looking leaves into the hole, arranging it so that the skull was lying in the middle of a green circle.

"You don't know it was a she," Stefan said.

"And you don't know it was a he," Amy answered, astonished at her own cheek in speaking to Stefan so sharply. He just grunted and scowled.

"That looks a lot better," Luise said. "I'm going to put my flowers in as well."

"Me too," said Tonia, beginning to throw the wax-white, golden-hearted frangipani blossoms into the small grave. "The petals are getting a bit brown round the edges, but I shouldn't think it matters if we're going to cover them all up."

"Let's get on with it," said Stefan. "It'll soon be time to go home."

"Shut up," said Luise. "We're going to say a prayer."

"The Lord's Prayer," said Paul.

"No," said Ian. "Ashes to ashes and dust to dust. That's what you're meant to say at funerals."

"Yes, that's right," Luise nodded.

"We'll say it three times."

Derek and Paul began scooping handfuls of sand over the skull, the garland of creepers and the fading flowers. Within seconds, they were altogether hidden.

"Ashes to ashes and dust to dust,
ashes to ashes and dust to dust,
ashes to ashes and dust to dust,"
said all the children together.

"Good," said Luise. "That was super fun. Now let's have one more swim before it's time to go home."

She started to run down to the beach and the others followed. Amy came last of all, still clutching her shell. She thought of the sand lying over white bone and dying flowers and found herself feeling cold in the flattening heat. She peered into the

tangle of green behind her, but there was no sign of a little girl in a torn pink frock.

Chapter 6

4 pm

"THAT BOY, HONESTLY" said Stefan's mother, shaking her head. "You can't take your eyes off him for one second. Where do you suppose he is now, when everybody wants to go home?"

"Ian and Derek'll go and look for him," said Mrs Robertson. "He can't be far away."

"There he is!" said Tonia. "Look, coming down from those rocks."

Stefan came running along the sand.

"Wherever have you been?" said Luise. "We've been ready to go for ages."

"There's no need to be cross," said Stefan. "I went back to get our towel. Amy," he scowled in Amy's direction and stuck his tongue out at her, "left it behind up there."

"I'm awfully sorry," Amy said.

"I should jolly well think so," said Stefan, smugly.

"Shut up and get into the launch," said Luise.

Stefan climbed in and sat down, holding the rolled-up towel.

Phut-phut-phut went the engine again as the launch made its way back to Jesselton. Gradually, slowly, the island was becoming smaller and smaller. Everyone was quiet now. Everyone was tired, dazed with the sun and the swimming and the food and drink. Stefan, Derek, Ian and Paul were right up at the front of the boat, looking out for flying fish, jellyfish, submarines, seasnakes or anything else that seemed interesting.

Tonia's mother was combing Tonia's wet hair and Tonia was squealing and groaning a lot. Luise was looking for a drink. Amy was all alone. She noticed the red and blue and white striped towel lying rolled up next to Stefan's hat on the bench. Without quite knowing what she was doing, but with the idea of putting the towel round her neck again as it had been for the Coronation, she spread it out on the bench. Something small and white and rounded fell out of it and rolled to the deck. It was the skull. Amy trembled with rage. Stefan hadn't gone looking for the towel at all, he'd gone to get the skull back. Great waves of anger and disgust rolled over her so that she could hardly think. How dared he? How could he? He was no better than a grave-robber. She had an impulse to shout at him in front of everyone, to disgrace him, to hit him . . . but she found the words sticking in her throat. But it *must* be buried, she thought. Somewhere. That poor little girl. Amy didn't like to think of the sand lying over her, but she must be buried. Amy picked the skull up quickly and dropped it over the side of the launch. It's perfectly all right to bury someone at sea, she thought with satisfaction. She watched it disappearing. Down and down it fell, through the translucent water.

"Ashes to ashes and dust to dust," Amy murmured although it didn't sound watery enough somehow. She glanced up to where Stefan was leaning over the side. He had his back

to her. Amy quickly rolled the towel
up and as she did so she noticed Luise
looking at her. Amy blushed. She saw
me, she thought. What will she do?
Will she tell? Luise smiled and put a
finger to her lips. No, Amy thought,
Luise would keep her secret and
Stefan wouldn't be able to say a word,
because then he would have to admit
that he went back and robbed
someone's grave, and even Stefan
wouldn't admit that. Amy looked
down into the water again. Could
there be ghosts under the sea? Now
she knew there was nothing to fear,
Amy longed to see the little girl again.
She had a sudden happy picture in
her mind of the child in a torn pink
frock sleeping gently under the waves,
with glittering fishes swimming in and

out of the floating strands of her hair.
Amy smiled to herself as they came
closer and closer to the white houses
and red roofs of Jesselton.

The Author

Stephanie Dagg lives in Innishannon, County Cork.

She is married to Chris and is mother of two children, Benjamin and Caitlín, and has been writing stories ever since she was a child. Originally from Suffolk, England, she moved to Cork in 1992.

Oh Gran!

by

Stephanie J Dagg

Illustrated by Kim Shaw

MENTOR

This Edition first published 1999 by

MENTOR PRESS
43 Furze Road,
Sandyford Industrial Estate,
Dublin 18.

Tel. (01) 295 2112/3   Fax. (01) 295 2114
e-mail: all@mentorbooks.ie

ISBN: 1-902586-62-X

Illustrations: Kim Shaw
Editing, Design and Layout by Mentor Press

Printed in Ireland by ColourBooks Ltd.

1 3 5 7 9 10 8 6 4 2

Contents

Chapter 1
News Time

'Has anyone else got any news?' asked Mrs Crowley.

It was Friday afternoon which was news time at school. Teresa Barry had just told everyone how she'd passed her first Tae Kwondo exam the night before. She now had a yellow-tip belt. (Frank Feeney, sitting in the back row, decided he had better stop teasing her in the yard.)

'Surely someone has more news?' persisted Mrs Crowley.

No-one put a hand up.

Mrs Crowley's eye fell on Emily. 'Emily, have you got some news?'

Emily had, but she didn't feel much like sharing it.

'Not really, Mrs Crowley,' muttered Emily, wishing her teacher had picked on someone else.

Mrs Crowley refused to be put off.

'There must be something you can tell us about, Emily. Now, come up here and share your news.'

Emily knew when she was beaten. She shuffled to the front of the classroom and turned to face the others.

'My news is that Gran is coming to look after me this weekend because Mum and Dad won a holiday in a competition so they're going away.'

Emily shot back to her seat, her cheeks burning.

'Why, thank you, Emily,' smiled Mrs Crowley. 'That's nice news. I'm sure you'll have a great time with your granny!'

Emily and her friends weren't so sure. They talked about grannies at break time.

Oh Gran!

'Gosh, poor you,' said Mary Roberts. 'Whenever my granny comes she makes us turn the telly down so low that we can't hear it!'

'Yes, and my granny's always telling me to wash my hands and brush my hair and stuff,' groaned Dermot Halloran.

'Has your granny stayed before?' asked Niamh Desmond.

'Not for ages and ages,' Emily answered. 'You see, after Grandad died a few years ago, Gran went to live with my Auntie Hilary in Australia. Then just after Christmas she decided to come back to Ireland. We were going to go up to Galway to see her but I got chickenpox so we couldn't. But now she's coming down to look after me. She said she would pick me up from school today.'

Her friends pulled sympathetic faces. Grannies weren't considered cool.

Chapter 2
Gran Arrives

Emily was quite nervous when the bell rang at the end of school. To be honest, she couldn't exactly remember what Gran looked like! It must be more than three years since she'd seen her. Mum kept sending photos of Emily to Gran, but Gran never sent back any of herself.

'So how am I supposed to recognise her, then?' wondered Emily, annoyed.

She had a vague image in her head of someone small, smiley and rather wrinkly. But that was all.

She dawdled out of school, wanting to be one of the last out so that her friends wouldn't see her with her granny. Plus it would be easier to work out who Gran was if the other parents and relatives had already gone home with their children. But Emily's friends were curious about her granny. They dawdled out too so they could see what she looked like.

Glaring at them for being so nosy, Emily led a gaggle of her friends to the school gate. She looked across the road to where the remaining mums and dads were waiting. She recognised them all – except for a motorcyclist wearing a black leather jacket. So where on earth was Gran? Emily was dismayed. Mum and Dad would be at the airport by now. Gran was meant to be *here* to pick her up.

Emily looked at all the faces again. Had she missed Gran somewhere? Unless, no, surely not! Emily watched in amazement as the motorcyclist pulled off a tiger-striped helmet – and revealed the smiling face of an elderly lady. It was Gran!

Emily's mouth dropped open in astonishment.

'Where's your gran then?' hissed Niamh.

'I can't see a walking stick anywhere!' joked Dermot, not very nicely.

'Yes, where is she?' asked Mary.

'There! She's there!' croaked Emily, pointing to her leather-clad Gran.

Her friends fell silent in horror.

Oh Gran! thought Emily. I will never live this down.

Chapter 3
Biker Gran

Just then Gran caught sight of Emily. 'Yoohoo! Emily love!' she shouted at the top of her voice, waving madly.

'Yoohoo!' a couple of kids behind Emily mimicked, giggling. Emily went bright red and hurried across the road before Gran could embarrass her again.

Gran came up to her and gave her an enormous hug. Emily hugged her back. It *was* nice to see Gran again, after so long. Gran's leather jacket creaked as they hugged.

'You're creaking an awful lot, Gran!' observed Emily.

'Well, most people my age do,' shrugged Gran.

'No, not *you*, I meant your coat,' Emily explained quickly. 'It smells nice too.'

'Glad you like it. Now, come on, young lady. Let's go home for tea. I'm starving.'

Gran trotted up the road to where a huge, gleaming motorbike with a funny number plate was standing. A few children had gathered round for a closer look.

'Hey, that's a great bike!' said one boy.

'Yeah, cool stripes!' echoed a girl.

'Um, where will I go, Gran?' asked Emily, anxiously.

'Behind me, of course,' said Gran. 'I've got a spare crash helmet for you. Just make sure that you hold on tight.'

Emily wasn't sure she liked the idea of clinging onto Gran and zooming along. She'd seen people riding pillion on motorbikes and it looked really scary.

'I'm not sure Mum would let me,' she said doubtfully.

'Of course she would,' Gran reassured her. 'But we could walk home if you'd prefer.'

The children were still crowding round the bike. Here was Emily's chance to impress them! She shook her head firmly.

'No way. I'd love to have a ride on your bike!' she decided.

'Good for you!' smiled Gran. 'Let's go!'

Gran unlocked the big box at the back of the bike and fished out a bright blue helmet. She put it on Emily's head. Emily staggered with the sudden weight of it.

'Golly! It's heavy!' she protested in a muffled voice from inside it. When she spoke, her breath clouded up the visor. For a moment Emily nearly panicked – she felt as though she had an elephant on her head and she couldn't see! Just then, Gran pulled up the visor letting in a rush of fresh air and restoring Emily's sight.

'Phew! that's better!' Emily sighed. 'I feel like a spacewoman with this helmet on,' she added, giggling.

'You look a bit like one too,' agreed Gran. 'Now, you sit up here and I'll hop on in front of you. I'll have to push your visor down again.'

At least this time it didn't fog up. Gran helped Emily up onto the large padded seat behind her saddle. Then she climbed on in front of Emily, pushed the bike forward off its stand and turned the key in the ignition.

The engine purred into life, making the bike vibrate a little bit. Emily held on tightly to Gran.

'OK, off we go!' called Gran. She rolled the bike onto the road, revved the engine and kicked the starter pedal. The bike smoothly accelerated away.

'Eek!' squeaked Emily. It felt like they were going about a million miles an hour. Emily closed her eyes and hung on for dear life! Then she remembered that her friends were watching her. She didn't want them to think she was a scaredy-cat, so she opened her eyes again. Houses and people were flashing past. It was brilliant!

'Oh Gran! This is really cool!' Emily yelled above the noise of the engine.

'Isn't it!' shouted back Gran. 'Let's go for a spin before we go home, shall we?'

'Yes, please!' cried Emily. The engine roared as Gran accelerated again.

Chapter 4
Caught Speeding

F aster!' urged Emily a few moments later. They were now hurtling along the by-pass. Gran revved the engine.

'Even faster!'

Gran sped up even more. Both of them were so busy enjoying the thrill of the speed that they didn't see the police car parked just off the road, keeping an eye on the traffic. But the policeman saw them!

It was a couple of minutes before Gran became aware of the police car behind her. Suddenly the blue light on its roof lit up.

'Uh oh! Trouble!' she shouted to Emily. 'The police want to have a word.'

'Oh Gran!' cried Emily in alarm. Now they were bound to go to prison.

Gran pulled over and the police car stopped behind them. The officer got out.

'Good afternoon, sir. Please remove your helmet,' he said walking up to Gran.

Gran pulled her helmet off.

The man's jaw dropped when he saw it was an elderly lady underneath the helmet!

'Well, madam,' he said sternly, recovering himself quickly. 'I'd like to remind you of the speed limit on this road. You were exceeding it by 10 miles per hour.'

'Oh gracious! I am sorry!' gasped Gran.

'It's my fault, actually,' piped up Emily. 'I asked Gran to go faster.'

'Did you now?' asked the policeman, bending down to stare severely into Emily's face. 'Aiding and abetting, that is. Very serious.'

'Oh Gran!' squeaked Emily in dismay. Definitely prison.

21

The policeman's face softened.

'Don't ever do it again, young lady,' he warned with a wink.

'I won't, I promise!' whispered Emily.

'And the same goes for you, madam,' he went on, turning to Gran. 'No more speeding, you hear? I'll let you off with a caution this time, but next time – trouble.'

Gran nodded, weak with relief.

'On your way then. Safe journey,' smiled the policeman suddenly.

Gran and Emily drove off as quickly as they legally could.

'Oh Gran, that was scary!' shouted Emily, as they zoomed towards home.

'It certainly was!' Gran yelled back. 'I need a nice strong cup of tea to recover!'

Chapter 5
No Tea

B ut Gran was out of luck. Mum only drank herb teas these days and Dad only ever drank coffee so there were no proper teabags to be found.

'Goodness me!' grumbled Gran looking through the teabags. 'Camomile and eucalyptus, rosehip and blackberry, sage and onion – they must taste awful!'

'I don't think sage and onion is a type of tea, is it?' queried Emily.

'No, dear,' admitted Gran, smiling. 'I made that one up! But it wouldn't surprise me if your mum tried to drink it one day. So no cup of tea for me. Oh well, let's have a nice snack instead.'

'There's plenty of food,' said Emily.

'Mum went shopping yesterday.' She didn't add that it had been at the local health food co-op.

'Oh good,' said Gran, pulling the fridge door open and peering inside.

There was silence for a moment or two as Gran lifted up a few items for inspection.

'Tofu? Falafel? What on earth are they? Low-fat salad dressing, radishes, turnip, carrots, coleslaw, cottage cheese! Where's all the proper food?' she demanded.

Emily opened her mouth to reply that this was proper food and very tasty too, but Gran had slammed the fridge door shut and marched crossly over to the food cupboard. She didn't have much luck there either.

'Brown bread, sugar-free muesli, wholemeal spaghetti, tinned prunes, long-life skimmed milk! Is this what you live on?' she asked Emily, aghast.

Emily nodded.

'You poor, poor child,' tutted Gran, shaking her head. 'Come on, we need to find some nice healthy grease and carbohydrate. I'm taking you to the fish and chip shop for a real meal for a change!'

Gran grabbed Emily's hand and practically dragged her outside to the motorbike.

'By the way, where *is* the nearest chip shop? I've forgotten,' she asked, pulling her helmet on.

Now, there was one in the next village but Emily decided to forget about that one. The chips were always soggy there.

'I think we'll have to go to Burger Kingdom in town, Gran,' she suggested hopefully. 'It shouldn't take long to get there on the bike.'

'Burger Kingdom it is then,' announced Gran. She liked the sound of that. 'Does it do thick milkshakes and muffins too?'

Emily nodded.

'Excellent,' said Gran. 'That's where we'll eat from now on then.'

'Every meal?' asked Emily.

'If it does breakfasts too, then yes, every meal!' declared Gran.

'Oh Gran!' sighed Emily. 'That will be totally cool!'

Chapter 6
Lost on the Trail

Next morning found Gran and Emily tucking into egg, bacon and sausage burgers at Burger Kingdom. Gran had three paper cups of tea in front of her.

'What are we going to do today?' asked Emily, wiping ketchup off her chin with her paper serviette.

'I thought we'd go for a walk somewhere,' replied Gran, emptying a fifth sachet of sugar into one of her cups of tea. 'I looked at some maps last night. I thought we could drive out to the Derrybally mountains. There are lots of walks there.'

'Sounds fun!' smiled Emily. 'But what will we do for lunch? I could make us some tahini and tofu sandwiches.'

Gran pulled a face. 'No offence dear, but I think I'll stick to food that I can spell! I suggest we just stock up on muffins from this place and some cartons of milk. That should get us through till teatime when we can come back here.'

'Oh Gran!' Emily giggled. 'Mum would have a fit!'

So Gran went back to the counter and bought six chocolate muffins and six blueberry muffins for their lunch. She got four cartons of milk too.

Stocked up with goodies, they whizzed home and changed into suitable walking gear. Emily was a lot quicker than Gran, so she dashed to the kitchen to make a few healthy sandwiches for them both to go with the muffins. Gran's diet definitely needed improving, thought Emily to herself. She must be very short of vitamins living as she did on junk food.

Just then Emily thought of the very thing for Gran. There was a big packet of pumpkin seeds in the cupboard. Mum practically lived on those and no-one could accuse Emily's mum of being unhealthy. Emily shoved those into her rucksack too.

Gran appeared at last so they put their helmets on and headed for the mountains. It was quite a long drive and Emily was glad when they arrived as she was beginning to feel cold and stiff.

Gran unloaded their rucksacks from her luggage box and replaced them with the two helmets. Then they set off on one of the mountain trails.

'Goodness!' exclaimed Gran after they'd been walking for about ten minutes. 'That breakfast wasn't very filling. I'm peckish already. Can you get me a muffin please, Em?'

'Tell you what Gran,' said Emily, seizing her chance. 'Let's save the muffins for later. How about some nice pumpkin seeds to keep you going. They're very good for you.'

Gran pulled a face. 'Pumpkin seeds? Good for you? They don't sound it!' But when she saw Emily's earnest expression, she smiled.

'Oh, go on then, you health freak,' she teased. 'Just like your mum! Come on, I'll try those bird seeds of yours.'

Emily beamed and handed the packet over. Gran paled slightly when she saw the size of the bag but she bravely said nothing and took the seeds. She began nibbling.

As they walked along, Gran chatted away about Australia and all the things she had seen and done there. To Emily's amazement she seemed to be able to talk and eat at the same time. Emily especially liked listening to Gran talking about all the strange animals she'd seen – wombats, kangaroos, koala bears, duck-billed platypuses and kookaburra birds.

They were chatting so much that they forgot to concentrate on following the marked trail. They walked on and on in no particular direction until suddenly the path just stopped at the top of a deep gully.

'Goodness!' exclaimed Gran in surprise. 'I don't remember seeing this on the map.'

She scrabbled in her rucksack and pulled out the map. She pored over the sheet for several minutes, then she looked up at Emily with a worried expression on her face.

'I'm afraid we're lost, Em,' she said.

Emily looked around at the desolate scenery. The mountains loomed huge and menacing behind them. She glanced up at the grey sky which had gradually become more threatening without them noticing. She didn't like the idea of being lost at all.

'Oh Gran!' she sighed. 'What will we do?'

Chapter 7
Gran Finds the Way

'We'll have a muffin, that's what we'll do,' decided Gran. 'In fact, we may as well have a couple.'

So they sat and ate in silence. A pair of sheep eyed them warily but, deciding they were harmless, carried on grazing.

'Come on! Let's simply retrace our steps!' Gran suddenly announced, standing up. The sheep, startled by this sudden movement, trotted quickly away.

They found what looked like the path they had come along and began to follow it down, but it soon petered out by a little stream. Then they went back to their picnic spot and tried another path, but it led them round the corner and then gave up too.

'Hmm,' said Gran, thoughtfully. 'I'll have to try a trick my Aborigine friend taught me in Australia.'

'What's that then, Gran?' asked Emily, intrigued in spite of being pretty scared at being lost.

'You'll see,' smiled Gran, getting down on all fours. Emily gasped as Gran calmly laid her ear against the boggy ground.

'Oh, Gran,' she giggled. 'You do look silly! What if someone sees you?'

'Well, if someone sees me, we can ask them the way back to the car park can't we?' Gran pointed out.

Gran's words reminded Emily that they were out in the middle of nowhere with only sheep for company.

'What are you listening for, Gran?'

'Shh!' replied Gran.

Emily shushed. She fidgeted from foot to foot while she waited for Gran to do whatever it was she was doing.

At last Gran got up, a bit stiffly.

'That way!' she said decisively.

Emily shrugged her shoulders. That way was probably as good as any.

Gran strode along confidently. Emily hurried after her, conscious of the darkening skies and the chilly bite in the air. She hoped this *was* the way home.

Suddenly Gran stopped.

'What is it? Are we lost again?' gasped Emily.

'Just need to check the route,' Gran informed her and squatted down again to press her ear to the ground. Emily hovered anxiously. Gran slowly stood up.

'Are we OK?' demanded Emily.

'We're OK,' nodded Gran. 'We'd just begun to go slightly off course. This way!'

Once again Gran marched off, with Emily close behind. Emily wasn't sure but she thought she recognised a few features. Hadn't they seen a big rock like that one, shaped like a lion's head, at the start? And that clump of seven spindly trees on the top of the hill looked familiar, didn't it?

They rounded the crest of another hill – and Emily sighed with relief. There, glinting in the dim light of the afternoon, was Gran's bike!

'Oh, Gran!' she cried, giving her grandma a big hug. 'You got us back! You're brilliant. I thought we were lost for ever! But how did you do it? What did you hear when you listened to the ground?'

Gran looked guilty.

'Actually, Em dear, I couldn't hear a thing!' she confessed. 'I've never been able to, not even in Australia when my friend was trying to teach me to listen to the earth's vibrations. But I thought it was worth a try. And as it happens, while I was trying to listen today, I caught sight of some pumpkin seeds.'

'What do you mean?' asked Emily.

'I mean,' Gran went on, 'I could see your pumpkin seeds – the ones you gave me that I . . . eh . . . didn't eat!'

Emily's mouth dropped open.

'You see, Em, I'm afraid I thought those pumpkin seeds of yours tasted disgusting! I'm sorry, my love. But I didn't like to disappoint you when you were trying so hard to make me eat something that's good for me. So I pretended to eat them as we went along and dropped them on the ground instead. I got us home by following the trail I'd left! Luckily the birds hadn't found the seeds and eaten them. Or perhaps they're like me, and prefer muffins!'

Gran grinned as she said that, and dug some muffins out of her rucksack.

Emily didn't know whether to be cross or grateful to Gran for throwing all those pumpkin seeds away. She was also a bit miffed at being tricked by Gran over the ear-to-the-ground business. She'd really thought Gran had 'listened' their way back home.

Then she saw the funny side, and started to chuckle.

'Oh, Gran, you really fooled me,' she admitted.

'Yes, I did, didn't I!' agreed Gran, and they both laughed. 'OK, who fancies a burger?'

Chapter 8
Swimming Pool Surprise

It was Sunday morning and time for breakfast.

'Come on, Em, I'm starving,' called Gran. Emily was getting dressed.

They were about to set off for Burger Kingdom. Then Gran thought of something.

'Is there a swimming pool in town?'

'Yes, it's a brand new one. It's huge and it's even got a diving pool. Can we go?'

'Sure, why not?' Gran smiled at Emily's enthusiasm. 'Go and grab your togs, love, and I'll fetch mine. We'll have a quick splash before breakfast.'

'Yippee!' shouted Emily.

When they got to the pool they found a notice pinned to the door:

Pool closed for diving competition, 9.15-11.00am. Entrants to register at reception desk before 9.00am.

Emily was really disappointed.

'Diving competition, eh? Registration closes in . . .' Gran looked at her watch. 'Streuth! In two minutes' time. We've got to run, Em.'

Gran grabbed Emily's arm and dragged her inside.

'But Gran, I don't know how to dive properly,' protested Emily, thinking Gran wanted to enter her in the competition.

'No, but *I* do,' panted Gran, hurrying up to the registration desk. The man there was starting to tidy up his things and was almost ready to go.

'Hold it right there!' called Gran, and raced up to him. 'One more entrant for the competition here!'

The man sat back down again.

'Oh good!' he exclaimed. 'And what's your name, young lady?' he asked, looking at Emily.

'*She's* not entering,' snapped Gran. 'I am!'

'Eh . . . are you sure?' asked the man anxiously. 'Um . . . our other entrants are all quite young.'

'Is there an upper age limit?' demanded Gran, fixing him with a steely stare.

'No, of course not,' he admitted, looking uncomfortable.

'Good. Now, here's my entry fee. Please enter me. My name's Edith Kelly.'

The man dutifully scribbled the name down with Gran breathing down his neck.

'There we are!' he smiled wanly. 'Please be at the pool by 9.15. I'm afraid you've missed the warm-up session.

'I didn't know you could dive, Gran!' said Emily, trying not to sound doubtful.

42

'There's a lot about your old grandma that you don't know,' chuckled Gran. 'Now, where do I get changed, Em?'

'Over here, Gran.' Emily led her into the ladies' changing area. Gran popped into a cubicle. It was a good job Emily saw her going in, because otherwise she would never have recognised the person who came out, not in a million years!

This person was wearing a vibrant emerald Aquablade swimsuit that came down to her knees, a matching cap and fluorescent green goggles. And for someone who lived on chips, chips and more chips, Gran was in remarkably good shape.

'Oh Gran, you look amazing!' gasped Emily. 'Just like an Olympic medallist.'

'Thank you,' blushed Gran. 'That's the biggest compliment you could ever pay me. Right then, let's get diving!'

The competition began a few minutes later. One by one the divers climbed to the top board and dived gracefully into the deep pool below. They were all very good and everyone clapped like mad. Then suddenly it was Gran's turn.

'Now a late entry, Edith Kelly,' called the announcer.

Gran stood on the top board and waved to the crowd with a flourish. Then she walked confidently to the end and turned round ready to do a backwards dive. No one had done a backwards dive yet.

Emily sat and held her breath. She hardly dared look as Gran tensed her body and then flung herself backwards into the air. She did at least two somersaults and a sort of twizzly thing before disappearing into the smooth surface of the diving pool, hardly making a splash.

The spectators around Emily erupted into a frenzy of cheers.

Gran climbed out of the pool looking very pleased with herself.

'That was terri fic, Gran!' said Emily.

'I was slightly off vertical when I hit the water,' sighed Gran. 'I'm a bit rusty.'

Emily looked at her in admiration.

'Oh Gran, you were fantastic and mega and brill and incredible and . . . and . . .' She was lost for words!

'Thank you, Em,' smiled Gran. 'I hope the judges agree.'

They did. She was the winner by a clear five points. There was thunderous applause as she went up to receive the trophy followed by a great gasp as she peeled off her cap and goggles and everyone realised that she was an elderly lady!

'Oh Gran,' chuckled Emily. 'You're a real winner!'

Chapter 9
News Time Again

It was Monday morning. News time. Frank Feeney was telling a rather boring story about what had happened to him over the weekend. Emily wasn't listening.

'Thank you, Frank,' said Mrs Crowley. 'Now, Emily . . . Emily! How did you get on with your granny? Come and tell us!'

Emily stood up in front of her class.

'On Friday we went for a motorbike ride and Gran got stopped for speeding. Then on Saturday we got lost going for a walk but Gran got us back by listening to the ground like Aborigines do! (Emily decided not to mention the pumpkin seeds.) On Sunday Gran won a diving championship. *And* we ate every meal at Burger Kingdom.'

Emily looked at her friends in triumph. They were all staring back at her with a mixture of total amazement and envy. Even Mrs Crowley looked astonished.

Oh Gran! thought Emily proudly. It's brilliant having the coolest Gran around.